THE MAGIC
HOCKEY
STICK

To our
parents

Raymond

Felicia

Joseph

Jean

Peter Maloney

PUFFIN BOOKS
Published by the Penguin Group
Penguin Putnam Books for Young Readers,
345 Hudson Street, New York, New York 10014, U.S.A.
Penguin Books Ltd, 27 Wrights Lane, London W8 5TZ, England
Penguin Books Australia Ltd, Ringwood, Victoria, Australia
Penguin Books Canada Ltd, 10 Alcorn Avenue, Toronto, Ontario, Canada M4V 3B2
Penguin Books (N.Z.) Ltd, 182-190 Wairau Road, Auckland 10, New Zealand
Penguin Books Ltd, Registered Offices: Harmondsworth, Middlesex, England

First published in the United States of America by Dial Books for Young Readers,
a division of Penguin Putnam Inc., 1999
Published by Puffin Books, a division of Penguin Putnam Books for Young Readers, 2001

10 9

Copyright © Peter Maloney and Felicia Zekauskas, 1999. All rights reserved

THE LIBRARY OF CONGRESS HAS CATALOGED THE DIAL EDITION AS FOLLOWS:
Maloney, Peter, date. The magic hockey stick/Peter Maloney and Felicia Zekauskas.—1st ed.   p.   cm.
Summary: When her parents win Wayne Gretsky's hockey stick at a charity auction,
a young girl begins playing with it and becomes her team's star.
ISBN 0-8037-2476-4   [1. Hockey—Fiction. 2. Gretzky, Wayne, 1961- —Fiction. 3. Stories in rhyme.]
I. Zekauskas, Felicia. II. Title.   PZ8.3.M31045Maj 1999   [E]—dc21   99-17201   CIP

Puffin Books ISBN 0-14-230015-2   Manufactured in China

The illustrations were created in pencil and gouache.

PUFFIN BOOKS

THE MAGIC HOCKEY STICK

AND Felicia Zekauskas

Mom never knew why she was sent
Two tickets to go to that "special event."
She just said to Dad, "It's for a good cause . . .
And charity auctions are always such draws!"

My father said, "Honey, you've got to be kidding—
We haven't the money for auctions or bidding!"
But that Friday night, tuxedoed and gowned,
My mom was all smiles while Daddy just frowned.

They went to that auction and kept their hands low,
'Til Mother reached up to straighten her bow.

The auctioneer spotted her hand in the air,
And shouted out, "SOLD! to the woman back there!"

My father blacked out and when he awoke,
He looked up at Mom and said, "Are we broke?"

All she could say was, "It happened so quick—
And now we're the owners of Wayne Gretzky's stick.
It might not be something that you would have bought her,
But think of the joy it will bring to your daughter!"

At breakfast Mom asked if I could explain,
How great was this Gretzky, this player named Wayne?
I told her that Wayne was the best of all time
And how he just scored goal nine-ninety-nine.

Then Dad butted in, "Let's make one thing clear—
This stick's not a toy, it's not to leave here.
It cost us a fortune, so please don't you take it—
I'd go through the roof if someone should break it!"

But one day the pull of that stick got too strong,
And though what I did was terribly wrong—

I took down that stick with Wayne's autograph,
And hid it inside of my long-necked giraffe.

I went to the rink and down to the ice,
Where some people pointed and others looked twice.
Even my teammates had a good laugh—
I must have looked odd with that old stuffed giraffe.
But out on the ice on my very first shift
I suddenly knew that I had a great gift.

As soon as I touched it, I wasn't the same.
That stick changed my style, it changed my whole game.
And as my first shot whizzed past the goalie,
I heard him exclaim, "Gee whiz, holy moly!"

Nobody noticed the name on my stick,
But that very day I scored a hat trick!

I'd sneak the stick out whenever we played—
I can't even count all the goals that I made.
I'd always score once, and more often twice.
That magical stick was quite a device.

Then after each game I'd sneak the stick back.
Thank goodness my parents weren't ones to keep track!

But while I was having this fabulous season,
Wayne had stopped scoring and I knew the reason.
Game after game he just couldn't score:
One game, then two games, then three games, and more.

Waning Star?
The Great One Stalls at Goal #999

GRETZKY SCORELESS AGAIN
AND AGAIN AND AGAIN

ALL THE DIRT THAT WE CAN DIG U

New York — Is Wayne Gretzky, hockey's "Great One," washed up? Gretzky hasn't scored in 17 straight games, the longest

SLUMP

I read all the papers, the writers were rough—
They wrote that Wayne Gretzky had lost his best stuff.
They said that old Wayne, once so great and admired,
Was now just too slow, too old, and too tired.

Oh, how I fumed to hear such things said—
I tossed and I turned and I writhed in my bed.

And then as I fell into deepening slumber,
A voice said to me: "RETURN THE MAN'S LUMBER."

That stick meant the world to me and my team,
But who could ignore such a voice in a dream?
And then I remembered that warning from Dad—
If that stick should vanish, he'd really be mad!

But I didn't care—I'd made my decision.
I knew what to do, I now had a mission:
I'd go to the Garden and ask to see Wayne.
I knew I had something to ease all his pain.

The man at the door was a fellow named Bob,
And letting me in could have cost him his job.
But he was a fan as well as a guard.
He told me, "Be kind, Wayne's taking this hard."

Wayne was way down, way down in the dumps.
"It's bad," he said sadly, "the worst of all slumps."
Then I took the stick from my trusty giraffe:
Wayne saw it was signed with his own autograph.

I said, "It's the stick that scored nine-ninety-nine,
I want you to have it, it's not really mine.
It's made me much better, I'm now my team's star—
I'm sure it will bring out the star that you are!"

Now, Wayne always welcomed a timely assist,
So he laid his strong hand on my little girl wrist—
"But what about you, girl, this stick helps you score."

But I said that I thought that he needed it more.
He said, "You're most kind," and then with a laugh,
The Great One asked me for *my* autograph.

Later that night I watched ESPN:
The Rangers and Gretzky were playing again.
Then Dad called to me, "Come in here quick!
Tell me, young lady: Just where is that stick?"
I said, "Dad, I'm sorry, but please come with me."
And I sat him in front of our color TV.

As we looked on, The Great Gretzky scored.
And seeing that stick, my father just roared:
"You gave him OUR stick, for crying out loud!"
But Mom slapped me five and said she was proud.
"Wayne may have scored with a flick of his wrist,
Yet it was our daughter who gets the assist!"

In our final game we played well and won,
Still I was more pleased with what I had done.
I had pulled Wayne right out of his slump,
And helped him get over the thousand-goal hump.

And as for that stick and how much it's worth,
It's now the most famous stick on the earth.
It's up in Toronto encased in a shrine,
That stick with two names: Wayne Gretzky's and mine.

THE
END